D1558850

MORNING
PAPERS

KATHY MARSHALL

The pages that follow are called "morning papers".

My wise sister-in-law, Carol, shared this idea with me many years ago.

It has continually crept back into my thinking as more than a good idea, but one I need to begin.

The challenge is to just start writing, with no formed thoughts, necessarily, when you first sit down.

I have suppressed it with some unknown fear… maybe that I really don't have anything to say, but I'd rather pretend I do, and "just don't have time to put it down". And writing is not something I have training, or therefore confidence, in….

But I am motivated by two things:

1. I want to live more aware of the broader scope of things in this world, and the one to come, as well as, of the people in my life, and my own honest reactions, feelings, and thoughts. I have a suspicion that they are in there somewhere.

2. I want to have some of our family's stories, memories, and words noted, like the memorial stones God told Israel to collect, in order to recall his faithfulness. What better time, than now, as I watch our family grow? I am in the middle of 4 active generations, and stories are any family's heritage!

So, with the encouragement of Randy, and of our daughter, Whitney, this morning, I am telling the devil that I am turning my ears

off to his whispers of failure and
hesitation, and just starting!

Fingers on the keyboard...let's go
and try this thing out!
I'm not jumping over the grand
canyon after all.
How scary can it be?!

A Lucy Heart

I have realized that one of my main fascinations about the tales of Narnia, besides a complete enrapture over the lion, Aslan, is Lucy.

She is one of the 4 Pevensie children who was once one of Narnia's queens, brought into the magical land through a wardrobe.

She is the youngest. Starting with her fresh childlikeness (the best version of it!) She responds:

...in wonder to this place,

...in love with the unlikely characters she meets, and

...in full devotion to the lion who came to free them from the spell of the white witch, who had made the land to know only winter, but never Christmas.

I would love a Lucy-heart!
She is full of fresh awe, and lives out many adventures in great freedom, bold and gracious, wide-eyed, and trusting.

She knows that this lion could prompt fear and danger, but she knows him to be good. She trusts him, no matter what, even the ridicule of her siblings.

In that, there are points in the story where they follow her, as she follows Aslan, because only she can see him. And every year more that she knows him, he becomes bigger! How beautiful!

I love her flying to him when he appears, and nestling into his mane, unafraid, with full adoring.

He breaths on her, speaks to her.
She sees him and follows.

She takes the liberty of honest
wrestling's, expressing her heart, in
the uncareful way a child does.

She knows that in his appearing,
and in her closeness to him, all will
be well.
Aslan tells her that she will know
him by another name back in her
country...as do we. His name is
Jesus.

He came at Christmas, as a baby.

He broke the spell of sin and
death.

He will return as promised, and
make everything right, good, and
glorious!

As so, he bids us to follow, and strengthens us as we wait, just like dear lucy!

Breathing

It's one of the moment-by-moment things that happens that we largely take for granted.

That fact came into full focus when we had a grandson born with breathing problems and the 17-day NICU stay, and prayer vigil, which followed.

As the Lung Association says, "If you can't breathe, nothing else matters!"

To stop, ends life on this earth for sure.

So other than physically getting to continue by it, there might be something for the soul in breathing in...quiet, God's nearness, and being filled up when the hurry gets us down and ragged.

Ann Voskamp made a challenge to go for a walk and do only two things: listen and breathe.

Try it! It's actually hard, as so many thoughts keep invading our minds, stirrings, making plans, thinking about people and events, even the prayer list.

But to stop and breathe is wise advice.

Kari Jobe sings:
"Breath in, breath out.
You will find him here.
Come and rest here; there is refuge...now.

Find His peace.
Know I'm not alone.
I will rest in you."

I admit that this is not a bent or habit of mine. And our culture doesn't help a bit.

How do I look at this in wisdom's framework?

In the Garden of Eden, God "breathed into (Adam's) nostrils the breath of life, and man became a living being." This was in the beginning.

Then Job adds, "The Spirit of God has made me, and the breath of the Almighty gives me life."

Isaiah 42:5, "Thus says God the Lord, who created the heavens and stretched them out, who spread forth the earth and that which comes from it, who gives breath to the people on it, and spirit to those who walk on it." Daniel speaks of "God who holds your breath in His hand and owns all your ways."

Acts 17:25: "He gives to all life, breath, and all things."

"To the lawless He will consume with the breath of his mouth." …II Thes. 2:8

"Let everything that has breath praise the lord!" Psalm 150:6

This makes me a bit more aware of where it comes from, and to whom it returns!

That's worth a good walk, to pay fresh attention to this daily gift!

Circling In

I have prayed much over the years for Randy's travels and speaking. That is what he does, and that is what I do to come alongside. There is great effort being made just to "get there," wherever "there" is at the time.

He has said many times that his job is easy, but the travel is the real work! He could have two full days of travel to speak for an hour or so!

It's like so many things in my daily life as well.

The same principle is at work when I get up early to do this-or-that, and in about 2 hours I actually get to it.

I may actually start!

I circle in with all sorts of encumbrances to remove, needed items to gather, then the task of ridding myself of the pull against initial inertia!

I am sure it has much to do with my self-diagnosed attention deficit, but holy cow!

Why is it so hard to get to the main thing?!

It's either "just the way it is" in this world, or it's a discipline to fight through.

Or, possibly the "interruptions" might just be as important in god's eyes as the task at hand.

Only he can sort all thing's value and work his good in the whole of it!

Groan with hope

Yes, indeed we "groan in our tents"!

Jesus has paid the price for our sin and, by his blood, freed us from its penalty.

Amazing!

And one day, in his kingdom, we will be free from its presence all together!

Glory!

But here and now, we battle its tug, it's continual ruin,
And the death it always results in.

The effects of our sin, and others, still plays out in our day to day lives.

Ugggg!

As I live in my own skin, I long for the day of Christ's return.

As I love "my household," my heart all wrapped up in their unfolding stories, I observe, that what we feel is exhaustion, but what is seen (deep down real) is beauty.

By the thoroughness of Christ's redemption and the multi-faceted wonders of his continual saving...

All hardship to those whom he has claimed is transformation.

He never wastes pain!

I think of the illustration of the little boy whose heart broke to see the caterpillar struggling so desperately to get out of the cocoon that he gently cut him free.

But because the little critter's fight to get out was cut short, he wasn't strong enough to fly, so he fell to a quick death.

Somehow, in the struggle, life and beauty will emerge.

We cannot understand, and it feels cruel, but....
Hope is there.
Good is promised.
The Lord is in it with us.
His grace is sufficient.

This is the "dot" on the timeline, and all that comes our way is part of making us what we will be for the long line of eternity.

We see dimly, but he is faithful.

When our faith is made sight, it'll all make sense!
Our rejoicing will have no end!

Knowledge

I grew up in a time, and in a family, where I got to really be a child. I was allowed to live longer than kids do today in naivety. I had some years that let me root in the loving care of my parents, free from many worries.

Add to that a bent to find fun and comforts, AND I am afraid I thought that learning would dampen my style.

I even prayed that God would not give me a "smart Husband"!

Oh my! A change in basic assumptions of a few decades!

I did get a smart husband and learned that it didn't negate fun and adventure at all!

I envy and draw from his knowledge as one of my main supports and graces in life!

And honestly, I moan the fact that I am not a natural student, short on enough curiosity to give myself to scholarship.

Even the things I do know now slip the memory!

My heart perked up when I heard Beth Moore say some years back, "Lord, please make me smarter than I am!"

Oh YES please, me too!!!

Early in my marriage I read the Narnia series by C. S. Lewis, and one of the characters was a real dolt...simple and stupid.

It was said of him by a wise professor, as an explanation of his lack of character, "he just hasn't read the right books!"

Well, now my love of learning is stronger than my habits of sitting still to do so, therefore I struggle still.

But I truly and deeply desire wisdom and knowledge more than any other riches! All you have to do is read the Proverbs, as one after the other paints a picture of the benefits. They have created a longing in this easily distracted heart!

"It is not good for a soul to be without knowledge." 19:2

"For the Lord gives wisdom; from his mouth come knowledge and understanding." 1:6

The Scripture links wisdom and knowledge, with wisdom being knowledge applied…the action that follows it, the truth worked out through the whole of that life, by a new way of seeing.

So, I have some running (and learning) to do to make up for lost time but am comforted by the words of James (Jesus' brother): "If any of you lacks wisdom, let him ask of God, who gives to all liberally and without reproach, and it will be given to him."

My Costly Life

I was sitting one day after some prayer...

The kind that resulted in peace, having felt expressed and understood.

What a joy!

I was freshly reminded of god's love, and that he heard me.

Then I realized that I had brought to him the needs of myself and many...asking for his help and healing, council, wooing graces, blessing, and rescue.

There's no shortage of things we need him to fix and make sense of. He implores us to come and ask.

It's a partnership with some power, and hope, attached!

We need. We ask. We need. We
need more. We need again...
Then I remembered, with a melted
heart, that Jesus (who lives to pray
for us now!!!) Was unmercifully,
illegally, cruelly killed, abandoned,
alone, misunderstood!

So that:

I would never be alone,
Never face death,
Live in hope,
Anticipate the kingdom,
Gain an inheritance,
Be filled with his own goodness,
And bask in unfailing love!

Oh dear! I don't think often
enough about Jesus' crazy, awful,
painful, shame-laden death, and
what his finished work means!

"Lord may this demonstrated love
be the motivation for my whole life.

I only have it because you laid down yours!"

Religion Lacks the Draw

I am all for doctrine! Without the sure foundation of theology there is no sure footing, no framework, no substance. It instructs my mind, assures my heart, and gives the rails to run on....

...but fails to give the fuel, the motivation, the life within.

Jesus came to be just that!

He links us to God and makes us his.

He identifies with us because he walked here as we do.

He connects the dots of the amazing love of God for us,

Shows us what he is like, is seen and known by his spirit who calls to us...beckons, enlivens!

We can't separate the substance
of our faith from the source, from
the object, the centerpiece!

The driving forces of our lives are:
To be enjoyed
To be fascinated
To gaze on beauty
To be someone great
To experience intimacy without
shame
To be wholehearted
To make a deep and lasting
impact

Those are experiential terms.
They wake up the senses,
Free us to be honest with those
desires and pursuits,

Indulge in grasping beauty, not
dismissing it,

To be known without fear,
Savor being loved,

Daring to get involved and bear
some fruit,

And stay amazed at real life stirring
in my own fickle soul!

Open my eyes, spirit of the living
God!
Herein I am satisfied in you.

Stillness

We seem to applaud those who live at a fast pace, nostrils flared, breathless in their busyness.

Is the assumption that if we are busy then we are important? We may deceive ourselves with that notion.

I am leaning into what it might mean to rest, to be still long enough to really see, really hear, awakened to wonder.

The frazzled life has fading attractiveness, with a longing to see what it might be like to live in awe a bit more, to be present for each activity, engaged, rather than looking ahead to what is next and hurrying to it.

The Bible speaks of diligent work, and also "dwelling in the land and cultivating faithfulness."

A quieter life, out of a stilled and nourished spirit might lend itself to being more spontaneous with time and possessions held more loosely, ready to give.

This is not inactivity. It is alive and responsive to the impulse of god's lead. It cultivates relationships, makes memories, expresses creativity, is faithful with responsibilities...

It's busy too, but freckled with pauses, sprinkled with laughter, taking time to think.

I love for a rhythm that includes stillness. I still desperately want to be productive, focused, and useful, but not to the exclusion of holy moments, refueling, leisure and laughter!

Oh, for the wisdom needed!

The Right Hand

Having a right hand that is preoccupying my mind these days (treated for gout, but it is more likely "Reactive arthritis") …all painful, expensive, and annoying…has made me think of all the references to right hands in our literature, folklore, and scripture:

We make Right turns.

We raise our right hand in making oaths.

We call someone valuable our "right hand man."

Then, most certainly, Jesus "sat down at the right hand of the father."

"At his right hand there are pleasures forever more" (Ps. 16:11)

"He is at the right hand of the poor" (Ps 42 or 43)

I LOVE this picture!

There is a precious link here.

Jesus is at our right hand, and HE is at the right hand of the father...just another snapshot of his bringing us into the fellowship of the triune godhead!

Your Heart is Showing

Lots of things tell the story of who we are on the inside…. Facial expressions, energy (or lack of it), priorities, actions and "works."

Even "a child is known by his doings," the proverbs tell us.

The Bible says that where our treasure is our heart will be also. So, our bank ledger is a real give-away of the values we hold dearest.

I have noticed that one other telling sign is what we laugh at and what makes us cry!

We can think of the cartooned villain in any story who cynically laughs at another's demise, contrasted to laughter that expresses pure delight in the one you are with…a "happy spill"!

There is nothing, by the way, more attractive and more free! Absolutely beautiful!

Equally attractive, and endearing, is one who is enough other-centered to cry their own tears over a loved one's pain and sorrow. It's a picture of the purest humility. We so tend to take everything immediately into our world, our needs and our experiences and thoughts...that odious comparison that does not fit here!

My three girls (both daughters and daughter-in-law) cry and laugh easily. It is one of the most attractive things about them. They have moaned before about how quickly their tears come, somehow embarrassed by it...but it is truly a sign of LIFE!!! They cry about truth and for others. They laugh with us, not at us. Deeply precious and life-giving!!!

Randy is reading a book that contains a comment I want to share:

"When I talk about the work these days, I sometimes get frustrated when I choke up. But I have never been happier in my life, and neither has (my wife). I told her long ago, "I simply have to be a part of something that makes me cry when I talk about it."

The man who led Randy to Christ, along with his wife, have lead marriage conferences for decades now. They were the first who we heard present such instruction, and it was during our own courtship and engagement. I could not give the outlines right now of the content shared, but I do

remember he could not speak his wife's name without tears.
THAT is what I remember.
THAT is what endears me to him.
THAT speaks volumes!

Frederick Buechner said, "Pay attention to the things that bring a tear to your eye or a lump in your throat because they are signs that the holy is drawing near."

I began a few years ago asking God to help me cry and laugh more. They, to me, would be signs of more love and freedom and less analysis, less "control."

I long for it still!

When directed at the right things, they both are visible expressions of truth running through a soul, a healthy perspective on things, getting outside of our natural selfishness, and splashing outwards

into the best of shared experiences
marked by love!

My 100 Percent/God's 100 Percent

I'll just start with the conclusion:
God's 100 percent is a whole lot
more than mine!

The first three chapters of
Ephesians are all about what god
has done to save us...

Redemption through Jesus,
Salvation by grace through faith,
Bought at a high price,
Brought ~~near~~by his blood,
Christ the cornerstone, and the
mystery of it all revealed.

His 100 percent is our rescue...all
his work!

It is followed by the last three
chapters, full of our response to this
amazement, this new position and
deliverance:
To walk in unity, love, light, and
wisdom,

Exercise our spiritual gifts,
Stand firm in the whole armor of god,
Relate well in our homes, and at work, and with our friends...

It's both, but his is first!

At the feeding of the 5,000, the boys brought 5 barley loaves and 2 fish.

With it, Jesus fed the masses, with leftovers.

Only God.

Only he can take what we have and make it plenty, make it more!

He takes our 100 percent and makes it enough, makes it a wonder that reveals himself!

Faith must be believing he is always right,

Fully trustworthy,
Worth whatever the cost, and
Living in grateful amazement, free
and risky!

All in…100 percent!

Boxes

Well, I will have to work this out as I type...

I love order, so tidying up often involves boxes, labeled, and stashed.

I am a big amazon shopper, so boxes pile up.

Seems that every time I take steps to restore order to the garage, piles of boxes go out to bulk trash...good riddance!

This orderly business that I am hardwired for has, as everything, Two sides to the sword. In seeking harmony and rhythms, I run my day in sections and get stuck with certain things only being done in the morning, or accomplished only in afternoon hours, and get easily thrown by interruptions.

That is a box I want to break out of....

Plan, but "letting it flow" is much more of faith, freedom, and grace!

That rhythm is much more of a dance than a march.

I also weary myself in evaluation of others, as if I can know their history or can read their motives. It smacks of a critical spirit and judgment which has no place in this heart.

Nauseating really!

God can be as creative with their uniqueness as he is with mine.

To give them the same grace I have been given, cultivates relationships marked by acceptance and love, free from a critical eye.

And the boxes I put God in, are wasted energy. He will not be contained, and I don't want him to be.

He is God, and I am not...duh!!!
It calls for some appropriate fear, and absolute trust, knowing he is wild, unpredictable, wholly self-contained, and busting with power and holiness, beauty, and mystery!

Something in all this just might hint at the freedom that Christ saved us for.

He will see all things to their glorious conclusions, and alone is adequate for each journey.

Our days and our ways are his!

Can't see the beauty, be of any use, or dance with joy in a box.

Oh, to dare to take on the rhythms of heaven's king!

Free Speech

I must have been the inspiration for the "Chatty Kathy" doll that came out when I was incredibly young.

My mom used to tell me, "you don't have to tell all you know!" I was puzzled by that, feeling that everyone must want to know my thoughts on everything.

Well, no they don't, not then or now...

Our tell-it-all culture has made something extremely sick and harmful out of "free speech," somehow taking it as a green light to spew the ugliest of what is inside us, justified in doing so!

It is so rampant now that I would call it toxic.

Many years ago, Randy and I were at a dinner in a wonderful home, and the host was sharing stories not very flattering about his wife, who was at the table.

Playfulness was at the heart of it I think, motivated by entertaining us, but it grew uncomfortable.

I said, "do you want to say anything?" to her.

She smiled graciously, and their son said, "this family is held together by what my mom doesn't say!"

I have never forgotten that.

More power and more love by what is not said!!!

My son and my sister-in-law mirror the same influence in their wisdom. I have seen both of them on numerous occasions, sit silent.

When gossip gets out of hand. Most times, I know that they know more about the topic than those talking, but don't add any kindling to the small fire building.

Proverbs 21:23 says: "whoever guards his mouth and tongue keeps his soul from troubles."

And "where there are many words, sin is inevitable."

I have noticed that scripture has lots and lots to say about the tongue, and its power to bless or to curse.

James has some extraordinarily strong warnings about it, one being that "the tongue is a fire, a world of iniquity."

How we use it has meaning for the whole course of our life!

We might all do well to play the "quiet game" occasionally!

We just might hear each other if we did.

We might just find that the living and wise word of God, might eek into our souls and we could speak what is true and edifying.

It would change the whole world!

A powerful thing!

I best start with myself!

"Let the words of my mouth and the meditations of my heart be acceptable in your sight, O lord, my rock and my redeemer!" Psalm 19:14

Just do it!

We have gotten used to that phrase as one having to do with sports shoes, and the effort to win in competition.

The reason it sticks is that it is motivational and pithy at the same time.

Makes me think of other charged challenges, that somehow, we think by reading them, we are also doing them.

Start with familiar phrases (commands) from the psalms: "give thanks," and "praise the Lord"!

I read such this morning, and it hit me afresh to go ahead and do that.

Act on it!
Obey!
Practice!
Be specific!

Being told to give thanks requires obedience to it, an action step. Go ahead and tell God what I am thankful for...with my mouth, with words, with specifics!

I had a mentor many years ago tell me that to say "praise the lord" is not the praise itself any more than to say "shut the door" actually closes it!

How many things I miss by "just knowing" something and thinking the familiarity of it assumes I am a participant, a doer!

Ready to buckle up my shoes and take steps, get in the game!

Just do it!

Laugh or cry

Have you ever noticed how closely they run together?
Many situations call for one, or the other, and it almost doesn't matter which one.

Wasn't it Shelby in steel magnolias that is famous for declaring "laughter through tears is my favorite emotion?

My girls do a lot of both, and it is one of the things I love about them. They think they need to have their tear ducts snipped to stop the flow, but I assure them (as my mom did me) that tears are a sign of life!

They really are!!!

To feel deeply has its expression, and what you feel often reveals itself in crying. It is then a telling sign about what you value most, what moves you with compassion, what fears you harbor, what gratitude you feel, what tenderness's you share.

Let it speak!

And oh laughter! So similar really and proven to be profoundly healthy (lots of science about it, but I don't do science!). When our son was dating Julia, he told us she laughs all the time. I told him it was a "happy spill."

An overflow of the heart, a sign of her new and gurgling love! The thing I love most about our family is easy laughter.

It's our best therapy!

I used to tell our kids when they argued, and were put-out with each other, mad and blaming, that they had to face each other and stay until they could hug or laugh.

It always ended in giggles that set the tone for the rest of their play time, until a reset was needed again.

Abraham Lincoln said, "with the fearful strain that is on me night and day, if I did not laugh, I should die."

True truth even in the war room, in the white house!

Give unapologetic expression to the life of your soul!

Remedies

Since the original sin in the Garden of Eden, when man's perfect relationship with God was broken, ruin and decay began to mark everything... truly everything!!!

I hate it when things don't just work as they are supposed to! Think how much time, energy, and money are spent daily on trying to get things repaired, or at least improved.

This uphill, discouraging, and constant effort has to be part of why we long for the time when Jesus comes to reign!

Much of my life, it seems, is scheduling repairmen to fix broken things, to restore items to full function, to give them a bit more life.

Add to the domestics, our toys and appliances, our own vanity, and the search for products to repair the spiral downward, to correct, cure, and cover!

I thrill at anything that turns confusion into clarity, and what is inefficient into efficiency, what is lacking, made whole!

It's renewal that I long for!

New life is so attractive and so deeply encouraging, even in the little stuff…

Sometimes just a taste of it lets me hang on, looking ahead to everything being made right…

Everything sad made happy…

Everything broken made whole.

That is the work of our master Jesus, and one day we'll see the glorious conclusion!

Remembering

Remembering, "calling to mind," are surely the activities of a happy heart.

Of course, it has to be the recall of happy, good, and edifying things for that to be true!

First the bedrock of true truth! Start there!

Those recalled absolutes, assurances, and promises to go a long way in replacing the things that no longer need to be remembered, just like God who "remembers our sin no more...casting it as far as the east is from the west!"

So, part of therapeutic remembering is healthy forgetfulness!

The richest things that families' shares are their personal memories/stories.

"Remember when...we smoked grapevine on our camping trip! Remember when Whitney, Stephen, and John David, pulled g'mama on the canoe?

Remember when we watch the firemen douse our burning home?

Remember when the kids' brought buckets of frogs into the house, in Destin, to scare me and Linny?

Remember when we all slept under the Christmas tree?

Remember when Whitney was left last at the Pi Phi house because dad couldn't get there due to car-trouble?

Remember john's three home-run game, beating Pearce?
Remember Mindy and JD's fun beach wedding?
Etc.!
Etc.!
Etc.!

That is the stuff that keeps tightening the threads around us.

Even some of the awful stuff, with the benefits of time and grace and retelling only become funny and unifying!

Talking about them, laughing together, keep them fresh.

Conversation and, of course, pictures, make our children remember growing up adventures that would otherwise be lost, left only in the past!

May it never be!

Pay the price!
Make the memories!
Continue the reunions!
Plan for togetherness!
Then, never stop telling the stories!
That is where I think we will find
God in our midst!

Recall and reflection, once we
step away, will keep telling our
souls that our God is writing our
stories, and he is using all of the
ingredients to knit his works into our
fleeting years here!

...foreshadows of the real
adventure that awaits when all is
made right!

Roots

I love to have flowers ready for cutting and sharing. They are a language of beauty and blessing to me... involving eyes, hands, and heart!

One of my favorite flowers to have and enjoy is coreopsis. That began when, my friend, Gaylan gave me a mason jar full of them for a picnic table arrangement many years ago. The bright splash of yellow whimsy has stayed a happy memory.

This past Spring, I saw that an established coreopsis plant in my garden showed new blooms as this perennial did its work.

I wanted more, so bought a new plant to grow alongside.

Even getting the same amount of water and attention, the young planting dried and withered soon.

Established roots made all the difference.

Nothing replaces time in establishing anything that will grow and flourish, bloom, and flower.

There is a visual lesson here to hold fast:
Stay the course, be diligent long enough to see life take on beautiful expression.

The Heart of the Matter

I am told to tend to my heart because the issues of life flow from it. That is pithy and clear, so it makes me think that since I know what it means (somewhat) that I am doing it.

In truth, I tend to many things, all the time, to the point of exhaustion, but generally leave the heart to just sigh through it all.

Even as I increasingly love Jesus, that too can be dutiful, respectful, well-meaning, but fall short of being "in love," lost in wonder, stretched out, and wholehearted.

He wants to be more than first. He wants to permeate all things!

And I want Him.

The parable of the Sower speaks of "those who hear the word with a noble and good heart..."
I want that.

The Proverbs are full of urgings to "apply my heart to instruction and discipline in order to gain understanding."

And out of a wise heart my "lips will speak right things."

I am to have a heart free of the envy of sinners.
I am to give my heart to observe wisdom's ways.

"as in water reflects a face, so a man's heart reveals the man." Prov 27:19

Ephesian's prayer is asking that the "eyes of our hearts be enlightened."

In some of the strongest emotion Paul tells the Corinthians "we have spoken openly to you; our heart is wide open. You are not restricted by us, but you are restricted by your own affections."

And of course, the law that sums up all the others is:
"you shall love the Lord your God with all your heart, with all your soul, with all your strength, and with all your mind, and your neighbor as yourself." Deut 6:5

So now I tend to it.
Cultivate it.
Weed and feed it.
Teach it to love what He loves.

It brings with it all the fears of getting it broken.

It probably will.

But his heart broke over our sin and all that separated us from the Father, and His love bought us back. And He will be with me until the end of the age, when we see His face!

Where else would my heart be so safe and secure!?

Voices in our Heads

We are new to having a sound system in our home and are set to learn how to save favorite songs to our playlists...

Embarrassingly behind the times!

Besides trying to choose the tunes that make our feet tap, or our hearts soar, we battle all the sounds we didn't choose constant advertisements, noise, news, and comments without end.

Then the tapes we play in our minds, often of lies, or just rehearsals of past hurts of disappointed dreams.

Our minds whirl!

It is exhausting!

Somewhere in this, we heed Jesus words as he taught the masses: "those who have ears, let him hear"!

Well, all those who followed Him could hear...but not all listened!

I want the ears that hear as Jesus meant it!

He will have to give them to me.

There is another voice speaking loudly enough for all to hear (at some level), and it is lady Wisdom, beautifully portrayed as a gracious and powerful woman in the proverbs.

We are told she lifts up her voice, cries out, by the gates, at the entrance of the city, and each turn in the road.

Her voice is to the sons of men!

We are charged to listen, as she speaks of excellent things. From her lips will come what is right.

She always speaks truth.

For those who listen, receive, and find Her, the promises are everything we truly seek!

Blessed is the man who listens to Her.

Those who hate Her love death.

Serious stuff! Tune in!

Back to basics

I have twelve grandchildren, and I have known all but 3 since they were born.

There's nothing like a new baby...precious and full of promise. As much as we might like to cuddle the tiny bundle, we would never want them to stay that way.

Growth is part of life.

Seeing them develop is the joyful adventure.

I just found a note I had made just under 6 years ago, asking God to help Sam and Bear learn to move (literally walk) and talk (communicate in order to say what they are thinking, desiring to be understood).

I must have been feeling their frustration.

It would be such a relief to them, and to those who listened to growls and groans instead of thoughts and wishes, to express themselves in words.

It happened, by the way!

I realize it's not so different for us as we learn to walk with Jesus, and to communicate with Him.

Out of that we too learn to express the love and hope we find there with others.

We never stop learning the basics, do we?

The words that capture me currently are:
Rest
Breathe

Come near
Walk together
Listen
Delight
We're not so different from a
toddler!

We are still learning the same
things.
Maybe the best we can do is hone
the skills and do them longer.... all
of our days.

Beam Blessings

When our house burned, and we
were about to rebuild,
It was suggested that we invite
people in to write blessings on the
exposed beams.

It was a new idea to me then and
was really fun.

We had most of our whole
extended family in town for some
kind of reunion, so many of my
most favorite people got to join in
the adventure, along with adored
friends.

It is now more commonplace.
We have been a part of writing
blessings on several homes under
construction since that time.

It is such a picture of what goes
into the core, along with the
strength of the foundation, being

the very things that the house is built on; the first steps of it being a home again, and what makes that place, that refuge, important.

Primary values are noted, and blessings are invoked, and they are there even when the sheetrock covers up the scribbled, but well intended, words.

They are like the truths being written on the tablets of our own hearts.

Tucked away, they are what come out of us when we host, worship, suffer, give, encourage, and bless others, just like we hope our home will do.

Forward Ho!

Nobody likes to be tripped up, set back, stalled, interrupted! I really, really don't!

...a dead battery, broken appliances, slow check-out-people, spills, pain that won't go away, lost keys, conflict, and on and on!

I think most of my prayers are against things that halt progress, which take time and money that I feel I don't have, and that generally derail life as I like it.... smooth and happy!

All the above is the way of this world.

It is the arena in which we now live. It's broken!

It's the groan that began in the garden, and it can be discouraging!

"but God" (one of my favorite phrases in all the bible!)

Has interrupted our fallenness...the backwards nature of things, the ruin!

Jesus came here, to reverse the curse of sin!

Sorrows will be turned to joy!
He will give beauty for ashes,
Make all things new!

Where there is lack, He brings gain.
When we are forgotten, He remembers.

From cursed, to blessed...
From loneliness, to being placed in his family...

Separated, but He tore the veil to make a way!

His purposes, even though now with tears, cannot be thwarted! Jesus will complete the good work he has begun, and we are moving forward with his unshakeable and eternal agenda! Life out of death! His truth is marching on!
It ends well!

Goodness

"Oh, for goodness' sake!"
Doing something just because it is
right and good makes sense to this
enneagram #1!

It has an appeal!

But guess what I know for sure?
Only God is good.

He says so!
Even as "the good girl," I know that
I am not.

"Oh my soul, you have said to the
Lord, "you are my Lord, my
goodness is nothing apart from
You." Ps16:2

The concept of goodness keeps
coming to me from various places.

Some friends and I are studying
Psalm 23, and most assuredly, with

the Lord as my shepherd, goodness and mercy will follow me every day of my life!!!

It carries the idea that God is so bent on blessing that He chases, pursues relentlessly, so that grace can overtake me!

How amazing!

There is a phrase that I have started every day with for several months...

It ends with "imagine the value of god's gift of the Holy Spirit, the divine distributor of the good things purchased by the Son, ordained by the Father."

His plan for us is good, even if it is "good suffering" or a season of "good hard" ...all of it is washed in His many assurances to make everything good in time!

"The Lord, the lord God, merciful and gracious, longsuffering, and abounding in goodness and truth..." Ex 34:6

"I would have lost heart, unless I had believed that I would see the goodness of the Lord in the land of the living." Ps 27:13

Every sin begins with a belief that God is not good; that He is holding back...

But truth is:
He is good.
He gives good gifts.
He gives them in good ways.

If Goodness is chasing me, I want to be caught.

Jesus' Face

In Isaiah 53:2 it is said that Jesus didn't have, in so many words, a handsome face, that we should want to look on him. I know that is in the bigger context of his coming in a humble way, not making his outward prowess the thing that draws fickle man.

But I have always thought that I would find it handsome.

"kindness makes a man attractive," as the proverbs tells us, and how lovely would a face be that is always gracious, tender, attentive, strong, and focused on mission?

As I write, one of the Christmas songs playing is, "Glory beams from His holy face"!

As Jesus has become more "beautiful than useful "to me (aka Tim Keller) the quickest trigger to my tears is now the thought of seeing His face!

"When you said, "Seek my face," my heart said to you, "Your face, Lord, I will seek"! Psalm 27:8

But now we "see as in a mirror dimly, but then (when He returns) face to face." I Cor. 13:12

That is the driving motivation to keep learning of Him, walking with Him, finding Him the treasure....so that:

There be intimate recognition when we do actually see Him, face to face, the veil lifted!

"Make your face to shine upon your servant and teach me your statutes." Psalm 119:135

Listen Here!

How many mothers and teachers say that very thing all day, every day?

"listen here"!

"pay attention"!

There are some important things for you to know, warnings to heed, instructions of all kinds, that you must take in.

I sadly remember lecturing my tribe, getting really tired of my own voice, and telling them, "stop me when I have said anything that makes sense"!

Constantly we can hear the chatter, the voices, the opinions, whether we want to, or not.

They bombard us.

But listening really is different that hearing.

I have always been amazed how many times Jesus said, "those who have ears, let him hear."

And that related to the Parables, with the mystery of the message given to some and held from others.

God the Father said of him, "This is my beloved Son in whom I am well pleased. Hear Him."

Proverbs 8 is a favorite. As I seek to put it to memory, increasingly, I am hearing how emphatic the plea is from "lady wisdom": "listen! For I will speak of excellent things. From the opening of my lips come right thing, for my mouth will speak truth." Listen up!

So somewhere in all this, there has to be a heart to learn,
A choice of what we give our full attention to, a teachable and attentive spirit, and stillness (that's the real radical one, isn't it?)

Good advice to stop and lean in... We might actually hear that "still small voice" that has much more to say than the loud ones.

Are you bent to listen?

Can you hear what is true?

"(The Lord God) awakens me morning by morning, He awakens my ear to hear as the learned." Isaiah 50: 4

"The heart of the prudent acquires knowledge, and the ear of the wise seeks knowledge." prov. 18:15

Preparation

There is a phrase I grabbed onto in a novel, I believe by Kate Morton. "Alice" was described as a "preemptive coper," known for her diligence and readiness in all situations that she had any control over.

I too love to anticipate events and possible wrinkles in plans in order to prevent unnecessary hassles. A drive for order does that to me.

As I sit this morning to write, it is Christmas.

It is a season of preparation...
decorating, giving gifts,
Hosting and attending parties,
cooking, and serving food.

Lots of tasks in readiness for the big day.

All the while we are rehearsing the story of Mary and Joseph having Jesus in a barn or cave, a humble place for the Savior of the world to be born...

With the carols reminding us to "prepare Him room."

Our wait for His second coming, His return, not as a baby, but the reigning king, is also a time of preparation.

We, the Bride of Christ, prepare ourselves, to leave this home, and go to live where He is.

All this time, He is preparing that place, with the promise to come again to take us to Himself.

We are to be ready.

"Eye has not seen, nor ear heard, nor have entered into the heart of man the things with God has prepared for those who love Him." I Cor. 2:9

Rose-Colored Glasses

When we were moving from the west coast to Texas many years ago, I was talking to my mom, and one of my sisters, who lived in Dallas, telling them how much I had longed to live near them. Allison made the comment "maybe you should stay far away. We look a lot better from there."

Talking to a daughter during some high school doldrums, she said, "Mom, I wish I could see myself as you do!" I wanted her too as well! I saw the truth of her beauty and sweetness when she only felt, at the time, sorrow in the struggle of it all.

There was a study years ago that was trying to find out the common denominator of happy marriages. Many dead ends resulted until that ahh-haaa-discovery was made.

Drum-roll please. Marriages that thrived were those in which the husband saw his wife as better than she saw herself. Rose-colored glasses! Idiosyncrasies were seen as endearing. He would not be deterred.

We have such a dynamic, as Randy sees me as who I really want to be, though in my eyes I fall so far short. I want to (get to!) Live out of his lens!

What a blessing!

Top it off with the astounding truth that God the Father sees His children (us!) Through the filter of His Son. I am seen as righteous in His eyes because of the righteousness gained in Jesus' rescue of mankind and has been imparted to me!
God sees me as he is making me for eternity...

Compete, holy, perfect, victorious, and beautiful!

Oh my! This is the pair of glasses I want to be seen with and use to see others!

No wonder I love roses!

"That's Mine!"

…what is?

What exactly is mine?

We kind of know that "we take nothing with us," but seem to still gather, and claim, and save, and hoard, and protect "our stuff." But the truth is I don't have anything that has not been given to me.

Not one thing!

"every good and perfect gift is from above."

And the God above has also promised to give us absolutely everything "for life and godliness."

I read recently that there is no word in Hebrews for "have" or possessing. It is all "to me."

I have not been able to let go of this concept.

To really "get it" would be an incredible freedom.

It would free me from wanting more than I have.

It would make me incredibly generous what has been given to me.

I would hold it all loosely, and I would receive it with exceeding gratitude!
All gifts.
All bonuses.
All from a loving hand.

I fear that we haven't come much farther than the children in our lives, clutching their toy that a sibling is threatening to grab!
How about a grand reversal?

"Here, take it. It was given to me
after all!"

Grownups maybe could mirror this.

It's not mine.
It's His, given "to me,"
To share,
To steward,
To enjoy,
To give away.

I think our hearts would open as
our hands let go of their grasp.

"Tov"

Every family has its phrases, and one that my siblings and I grew up with was "tov" .... tone of voice!

It was corrected as much as any action.
What's true in the heart is heard, no matter what the words are saying!

Randy and I laugh, as a perfect example, at a husband stating "yeah, I love ya" in a slack, distracted tone.

He may as well as save his words because they are not connecting to the one who really wants to be loved by him!

When our kids argued, I had them face each other to apologize. A forced "sooorrrry," with slumped shoulders and eye rolls, didn't do it either.

I moved to having them face each other until they could hug or laugh. Sometimes it took a while, but it worked! It got more to the significant part. The action, though waited on, was more of a step of reconnecting sweetly!

Dispute ended!

It hit me this morning that one of the reasons I love listening to a great voice read scripture is that it carries the tone of the passage and helps me get it better.

When Jesus says, "Have I been with your so long?!?!" It carries the frustration and more importantly the earnestness in His wanting to communicate that if you have seen Me, you have seen the Father. It's a pleading...

"please get it!"

Likewise in Isaiah 40, it is so endearing to read the word choices:

"Comfort, comfort (for emphasis!) My people, says your God (relationship!),

Speak tenderly to Jerusalem and proclaim to her...."
Freedom and forgiveness have come!

Randy teaches the communication process, and it is believed that 7 percent has to do with the words we say. The much bigger deal is how we say what we say!

I have found that I watch how people talk, more than I listen to their words.

.

It's not a great habit, but my spirit wants to know first, do you love me? Do you speak what is true?

Is there a heart connection to your topic?

Broaden the Scope

Most of life truly does start in our minds.

Prayer, grace, experience, sorrows, suffering, and the influence and support from the family of God, help move the truth straight… from our ponderings and meditation, into the heart…

And out of that "come the issues of life"!

All of that little process, by the way, takes all of our life to live out, and to realize it's fruit.

It also remains a mystery.

Randy and I have three children. They, and their spouses, are wiser than we have ever been.

Our oldest, and her husband are raising six children, and it is as they call it "a good hard" ...

Really good, as their adopted three are called acts of "pure religion" by the Apostle James.

It is close to God's heart.
Really hard because, well... It's hard!

On a great day... it's nuts! Pure and simple.

Whitney renewed this concept for me, of looking at the bigger picture... moving the scope out to take a broader, grander look at things.

I quote her, "if the promises of God, and the assurance of a glorious future, aren't true, we are crazy."

If a look at the Biblical teachings of Christ's second coming, and what awaits, doesn't do it, look at the visions God's spirit gave John in the book of revelation.

He says you will be blessed just to read this Book!

Indeed!

Prepare for dry-mouth-fear, astounding wonders, mind-blowing happenings, a powerful view of our merciful salvation, and an indescribable kingdom coming, that we are a part of!

With that healthy view of reality, we press on in the day to day, sights fixed on all that surrounds us, and is coming.

Gotcha Covered

Oh, how crafty I am at making sure I am covered.

I am working increasingly hard at it.

Getting ready just now, for the day, I got tickled at the efforts.... glasses to cover the eye-bags, shoe selections to cover the bunions, make up to try for a smoother surface,

Eyes to look alert, color for a sign of life, longer tops...you get the point!

Cover as many flaws as possible. Necessary, even if a bit futile!

A covering of sackcloth in the scriptures was a sign of sorrow or repentance.

Moses covered his face so the Israelites couldn't see that the glory had left his face.

God "spread a cloud for a covering" as one of his protective steps in leading His people through the desert.

Even from the beginning of my life, (God) covered me in my mother's womb"!

And the best yet:
"Blessed is he whose transgression is forgiven,
Whose sin is covered!"

God has us covered (as with a shield) …. from the beginning to the finish line,
And it makes all the difference!

It's in the Air

Are there places you go that you just feel something, where the very atmosphere of the place affects you?

It can be dark, gloomy, oppressive, and you want to flee.

...or it can be alive, possessing some kind of beauty that pulls you in and makes you want to stay, to savor it.

It's the basis on which we choose restaurants, or influences the things we do in our homes, all the while it's mostly immaterial, a hard to describe element that we seek. The literal feel of it draws us in!

I go to three grocery stores every Monday. I save the best for last. I start with the "warehouse," I move to a place for the pantry stuff, boring, but necessary. Those are rote and routine stops. I am thankful for what they offer, but nothing about them inspires.

They offer products without "life." My last stop, always savored, is where I get the fresh stuff. Both places I have in mind make me grateful for food, make me want to cook, and to eat well. There is a dynamic that has no real explanation, but a genuine reality.

People carry about them an "atmosphere" too.

Some seem to bring with them a dark cloud over their head, and their manner makes you come down a notch.

Some, by nothing specific, enter, and life gets better "just because"! It has to do with a life within the heart that shows on their face.

Open eyes give you liberty to be who you are, with acceptance as their calling card.

I have family and friends whose whole countenance invites you in. They are the ones whose company I choose, and those who get the best of my authentic and freely expressed self. I hunker in and drink it down.

What we know for certain is that in the Lord's "presence
Is fullness of joy"! An aroma of life unto life. More please!

One More Thing

When we are overwhelmed, tasks and demands are endless, and there is weariness of body and soul, we often begin a fierce elimination. What can I stop doing so that I have "more time"?

Even if you produce some things to stop doing, that too feels defeating and like failure.

Deep sighing!

In those seasons, this kind of evaluation is nearly impossible, because it all feels urgent, equally important.

Dizzying!

I am just back from time at the Eoff's, settling into a new house, with the swirling activities of a family of eight.

On a "good day," it's a circus. So much movement, so many words, so many places to be in various directions.

And besides just managing the clock and calendar, there's training, instruction, truth to impart "as you sit by the road and walk along the way"!!!

Hearts need tending to; not just schedules.

Help!

All there is burnout and exhaustion unless you add in the right things. Seems backwards, and defeating, but to stop and take a walk, take a bath, play a game, pray an honest prayer, linger at the table, watch a favorite show, laugh hard, work a puzzle, might just be the ticket to survival...

Or joy!

Teach us, Lord, your rhythms!
One of them includes rest…a
command, actually, because You
love us, and know what is best!

Your ways are perfect!

Ready Before Aim

Our kids gave Randy a poster one year of a man standing calmly in the doorway of a lighthouse, with the storm raging around him. He is in the "eye of the storm" unmoved. It profoundly hit me that he had to get in that safe place before the winds came.

He never could have fought his way to that place of safety unless he had been standing there in the first place.

Think how many situations in life have to do with setting your hope on what is unshakeable.... first!

Take your stand, commit your way, before it is challenged (because it will be!)

Many years ago, a friend invited me over to share something raw and painful, a confession.

I wrote a letter assuring her of my committed love before I knew what she would reveal to me. I took it with me.

It was a disturbing thing to learn, but the predetermined commitment is what held the friendship firm.

Our wedding vows are to be the same thing. They are a holy commitment. It declares that the marriage itself is about more than the couple...it's a picture of Christ and the church. It's the vow that keeps the marriage!

We just sent a grandson into surgery, after a previous one had gone terribly wrong. All the fears of the past experience came back to us. We worked through it together. His mama (our Whitney) said that as they drove to Dallas, the two of them confirmed that God loved them as much as he loved Moses, and his purposes for Marshall were as sure as for the Israelites...so they too would walk through the waters on dry, rocky ground!!!

Set your mind to what's true.
Set our hearts on whom we trust.

Let it hold us firm when all around it is challenged and hard.

Restoration

I hate broken things!

My biggest annoyances are when anything stops working as it is supposed to.

Furthermore, what I have noticed is that positively everything is broken. Just look at Genesis, chapter 3, and all of life moving forward, including my own "little black heart", that my grandmother asked God to bless!

When we moved into our newly built house after a fire, we, of course, got all new appliances.

"New" doesn't last long. As we just passed the 5-year mark, one by one, they all needed (expensive and annoying) repairs. The serviceman said that they are designed to break. How else would sales continue?

Worse is the broken nature of our society, with division and ruin, decline, and distrust...no elaboration here. None needed. We have made division lines in all the wrong places.

I need go no further than my own heart.

But there's hope, the renewal of all things is coming.

It is promised, by the One who never breaks His word!

Jesus, the rescuer, will complete everything that he began.

Revelation assures us that all things will be new, that is: fresh, not just second beginnings.

This renewal has already begun in the life of the believer.

A new heaven and a new earth are coming.

There will be no more death, tears, or pain...and everything that could threaten it will be defeated.

That's the best fix-of-the-broken we could ever imagine!

Rosy

One of the things I remember my mom telling me all my growing-up life was to "pinch my cheeks." My pale and freckled face needed some color.

Well, something about that stuck in the deep places of my mind because now, even where freckles have been replaced by wrinkles, I tend to my cheek-color with keen attentiveness! I have a dab of color ready to add at all times!

Somehow this struck a tender chord this morning as I read about the gospel.

Jesus began his ministry with these words," the spirit of the Lord God is upon me, for the Lord has anointed me to proclaim the "bisorah" (the gospel, the good news)."

So, the gospel was first spoken of in the old testament, and I am delighted to learn that it means, cheerful or joyful...rosy, fresh, filled with life!!!

The effect of the gospel has to be joy!

Being saved from judgment and given heaven as well is more than enough to give us joy every single day!

It is always fresh and must be freshly received.

Why, it's enough to make your life rosy-cheeked (thoughts from the Book of Mysteries, by Jonathan Cahn #132)

When our Mindy, a #6 on the enneagram chart, was engaged, her soon to be husband, John

David, said something that jolted us back to this same refreshing perspective. When our wonderful and emotional daughter would have a time of swooning, he would answer with, "but you're beautiful and we're going to heaven!"

I have loved that and have brought it to mind often since.

Receive this good news with fresh delight, and you will be rosy-cheeked...beautiful, and directed to our glorious, waiting home!

Take the Reins

For many years I have been impacted by a mental picture that Beth Moore shared in one of her studies.

It was in the context of trusting God with our lives...taking our hands off of it.

She said it's like taking the passenger seat and turning the wheel over to Jesus. Let your hair fly in the wind and be free in his good directions and thorough competency to get you to the finish line!

Who doesn't love a fast (safe?)? Drive in a convertible with no worries!?

Well, I have a new one.

Same idea.

It's current, as of a recent viewing of a Heartland episode, on Amazon Prime.

Amy is a horse girl, as I used to be. The love of horses has been rekindled in these ranch settings and stories.

She is in turmoil in trying to help her own troubled horse, as well as some accompanying relationship complications.

She has just spent some time in the home of a wise Indian.

During one of the nights, she had a vivid dream about being lost in the woods, completely turned around, as the trees crowded out any vision for a way out. It was a panicky scenario, leaving her bewildered and scared.

Tired of trying to make it all work on her own, there is a beautiful scene where she takes the reins and deliberately, places them on her horse's neck, in surrender. Her hands go up in the air, in release, with the intention of stopping her own strivings.

The balance of this picture, of our own trust in the living God, his word's council, and His Spirit's leading, we "give Him headship," as we stay on the horse!

We ride it out!

We stay on, find our way out of "forests" as only He can do, And enjoy the adventure!

Tied Together

Remember the old hymn "blessed be the tie that binds..."?

There is much more to say about that than I will do here, but it increasingly to mind that families have ties that connect them, that create a powerful unit.

They are meant to.

We have to remember that none of us chose our relatives.

Start with the providence, and subsequent many graces, of God. What is it that makes these relationships life-giving?

That make us want to be together, stay put no matter what?

I think it's our stories.

We are bound by them.

They hold us tight.

Most good things happen when we stay put. We don't flee when it gets hard, when we disappoint each other, when forgiveness is practiced.

Let the roots go down.

From them comes something beautiful.

Don't quit until they bear their most beautiful fruits and come to full flourishing!

Our stories include redemptive ones, hidden ones, shared experiences, belonging, protection, generosity, laughter, understanding, sacrifices, etc. etc.!

They can be recalled by just a word, a look, that no one else would catch.

They speak of that personal knowing, which sets us apart.

They are the private language of our family.

They unite us.

A message of grace results...to the praise of God!

Voices

There are so many voices! There is no rest from them.

It is inescapable!

Even checking email there are flashes of commercials running along the sides. Snail mail is like carnival barkers seeking to draw us in for the sale. The "news" I have come to hate, leaves us with more confusion that content...

And yet we can't avoid the sounds, the prattle, the noise!

Remember Eliza Doolittle singing "words, words, words, I'm so sick of words. I get words all day through, first from him, now from you..."

Simon and Garfunkel made famous the great invitation to "listen to the sounds of silence"!

Its why young moms love the "quiet game"!! Just hush for a minute!

During, and now after, the elections, I find myself wanting the nation to declare a day of silence.

Everyone stop talking. Breathe, listen, be quiet!!!

Then, we might hear the "still small voice of God," give ear to His whispers, let His written word sink into our souls and nourish us.

Proverbs 8 talks beautifully of Wisdom crying out, calling to the sons of men (read what listening to "her" voice promises!!!).

"Out of the mouth of babes and nursing infants (God) has ordained strength..."

"the heavens declare the glory of God."

And the firmament shows His handiwork.

Day unto day utters speech, and night unto night reveals knowledge.

There is no speech nor language where their voice is not heard.

Their line has gone out through all the earth, and their words to the end of the world."

Then the capstone, Jesus is called "The Word made flesh."

Let's listen to Him!

He, and his message, are unshakeable, utterly true, and completely reliable!

I am turning the world's voices and their volume down...maybe to mute!

Made in the USA
Columbia, SC
02 December 2021

50164475R00072